For Loraine & Mark

SIMON AND SCHUSTER
First published in Great Britain in 2013
by Simon and Schuster UK Ltd
1st Floor, 222 Gray's Inn Road, London, WC1X 8HB
A CBS Company

Text and illustrations copyright © 2013 Tim Hopgood

The right of Tim Hopgood to be identified as the author and
illustrator of this work has been asserted by him in accordance
with the Copyright, Designs and Patents Act, 1988

A CIP catalogue record for this book is available
from the British Library upon request

978-0-85707-749-3 (HB)
978-0-85707-750-9 (PB)
978-0-85707-751-6 (eBook)
Printed in China
10 9 8 7 6 5 4 3 2 1

PING & PONG
ARE BEST FRIENDS
(mostly)

Tim Hopgood

SIMON AND SCHUSTER
London New York Sydney New Delhi

Anything Ping can do,

Pong can do better.

Anything?
Yes, anything!

Ping likes ice-skating.

Pong does too!

Ping likes painting.

Pong does too!

Ping likes fishing.

Ping is learning to squeak French.

Pong can already squeak in nine different languages.

Ping decided enough was enough.

He was never going to be the **BEST** at **anything**.

So Ping sat down and did **NOTHING**.

"What are you doing?" asked Pong.
"NOTHING," replied Ping.

"Oh!" said Pong.
"I've never tried doing
that before. What do
you have to do?"

"NOTHING," replied Ping.
"Oh, I see," said Pong.

And Pong went off to
practise doing **NOTHING**.

Pong tried as hard as he could,
but he just couldn't do it.

Doing nothing was **IMPOSSIBLE**.

How does Ping do it? he wondered.

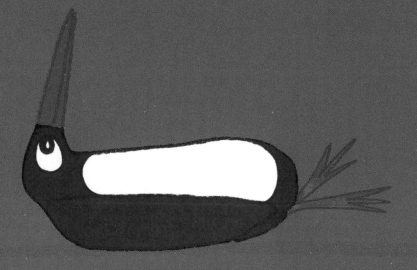

Pong decided he didn't like doing nothing.

But doing other things without Ping wasn't much fun.

So he wrote Ping a letter.

Dear Ping,
If you can spare the time,
I wondered if you would
like to come for tea?
I miss you.

Pong
x

Ping didn't open the letter straight away.

He was too busy . . .

. . . doing nothing.

Finally Ping read the letter.

He realized he missed his friend too.

The next day,
Ping made some biscuits.

And then he went to visit Pong.

Even though they were a bit burnt,

Pong said they were the nicest biscuits he'd ever tasted.

Pong had also done some baking.

TO THE **BEST** FRIEND IN THE WORLD

And, at last,
Ping realized he
was THE BEST
at something after all.